The BLUES Go Extreme Birding

Meet the BLUES

BING
Band Leader
Favorite color: Maroon
Bing loves:
- singing songs
- rhyming words
- using maps

Favorite expression:
"Let's cruise, BLUES!"

LULU
Blue Belle
Favorite color: Pink
Lulu loves:
- dressing up
- making friends
- taking photos

Favorite expression:
"Think pink!"

UNO
One-of-a-Kind
Favorite color: Orange
Uno loves:
- playing the guitar
- loons and rubber duckies
- and not much else

Favorite expression:
"Uh-oh!"

EGGBERT
Super Birder
Favorite color: Green
Eggbert loves
- watching birds
- reading about birds
- talking about birds

Favorite expression:
"Birding is the best!"

SAMMI
Sportster
Favorite color: Yellow
Sammi loves
- doing ALL sports
- getting a good workout
- going on adventures

Favorite expression:
"Girl power!"

By Carol L. Malnor and Sandy F. Fuller ✳ Illustrated by Louise Schroeder
DAWN PUBLICATIONS

For my husband, Bruce, with love — CLM

For W. Ellsworth again, and everyone who believes that extreme dreams do have wings. — SFF

For my brothers and sisters; I love you all. — LS

ACKNOWLEDGMENTS

The authors are especially grateful to the following people for helping the BLUES continue their birding adventures: Glenn Hovemann and Muffy Weaver for their creative and editorial skills, and Joseph, Suzanne, Camille, and Sophie Schroeder for their valuable "constructive criticism" and imaginative suggestions.

Special thanks go to Andrea Yocum and her 2010-2011 kindergarten and first grade students at Grass Valley Charter School in Grass Valley, California, and Karen Busch and her 2010-2011 first-through third-grade students at Living Wisdom School, Portland, Oregon.

We are grateful to Ed Pandolfino of Sierra Foothills Audubon Society for his assistance in assuring the accuracy of bird facts. Other important sources for bird information used in this book include *All About Birds* (Cornell Lab of Ornithology: www.allaboutbirds.org), *The Birds of North America Online* (Cornell Lab of Ornithology and the American Ornithologists' Union: http://bna.birds.cornell.edu), *The Life of Birds* by David Attenborough (PBS), and *Extreme Birds: The world's most extraordinary and bizarre birds* by Dominic Couzens.

LIBRARY OF CONGRESS CATALOGING-IN-PUBLICATION DATA

Malnor, Carol.

The Blues go extreme birding / by Carol L. Malnor and Sandy F. Fuller ; illustrated by Louise Schroeder. -- 1st ed.

p. cm.

Summary: Five little bluebirds go on a birdwatching trip to find and admire the world's record-setting birds, such as the fastest diving (peregrine falcon), longest migrating (arctic tern), and best mimic (superb lyrebird).

ISBN 978-1-58469-133-4 (hardback) -- ISBN 978-1-58469-134-1 (pbk.) [1. Birds--Fiction. 2. World records--Fiction. 3. Bird watching--Fiction. 4. Bluebirds--Fiction. 5. Voyages and travels--Fiction.] I. Fuller, Sandy Ferguson. II. Schroeder, Louise, ill. III. Title.

PZ7.M29635Bme 2011

[Fic]--dc22

2010031036

Manufactured by Regent Publishing Services, Hong Kong,

Printed January, 2011, in ShenZhen, Guangdong, China

10 9 8 7 6 5 4 3 2 1

First Edition

Book design and computer producton by Patty Arnold, *Menagerie Design and Publishing*

DAWN PUBLICATIONS

12402 Bitney Springs Road

Nevada City, CA 95959

530-274-7775

nature@dawnpub.com

We're the BLUES! A band of birds who like to sing! Sammi loves sports. When she read about the X-Games in *Birding News*, she couldn't sit still.

"I really want to enter an extreme event," Sammi sang, "but I don't have a clue what to do."

Back inside the Clubhouse, Eggbert said, "Hey, Sammi, after our last bird-watching trip you wanted to see more record-setters, like the bird that flies fastest or dives deepest. If we travel around the world to visit extreme birds, maybe you will discover your X-Games event."

"EXCELLENT!" sang Sammi. "I'll start packing my gear!"

Lulu announced, "I want to see the pinkest bird most, but I promise to take pictures of every bird."

Bing unfolded a map and together we made a list of world champions we wanted to see. The fastest-moving bird was at the top.

"Ready, BLUES?" Bing asked. "On your mark, get set, GO!" He blew his whistle and our EXTREME birding trip began.

Climbing with suction cups, Sammi led us straight up a skyscraper in New York City. Whoosh! A Peregrine Falcon dived past us at almost 200 miles an hour.

"Wow," exclaimed Bing. "Who would have guessed the world's **fastest-moving bird** lives here?"

"Look at the shape of those wings," marveled Eggbert. "Watch out, pigeons and starlings! You're his prey!"

Sammi sighed sadly. "I'm afraid my wings won't let me dive like that."

"Don't worry," Eggbert reassured her. "We'll see lots of birds, each with a different skill. You'll find your event."

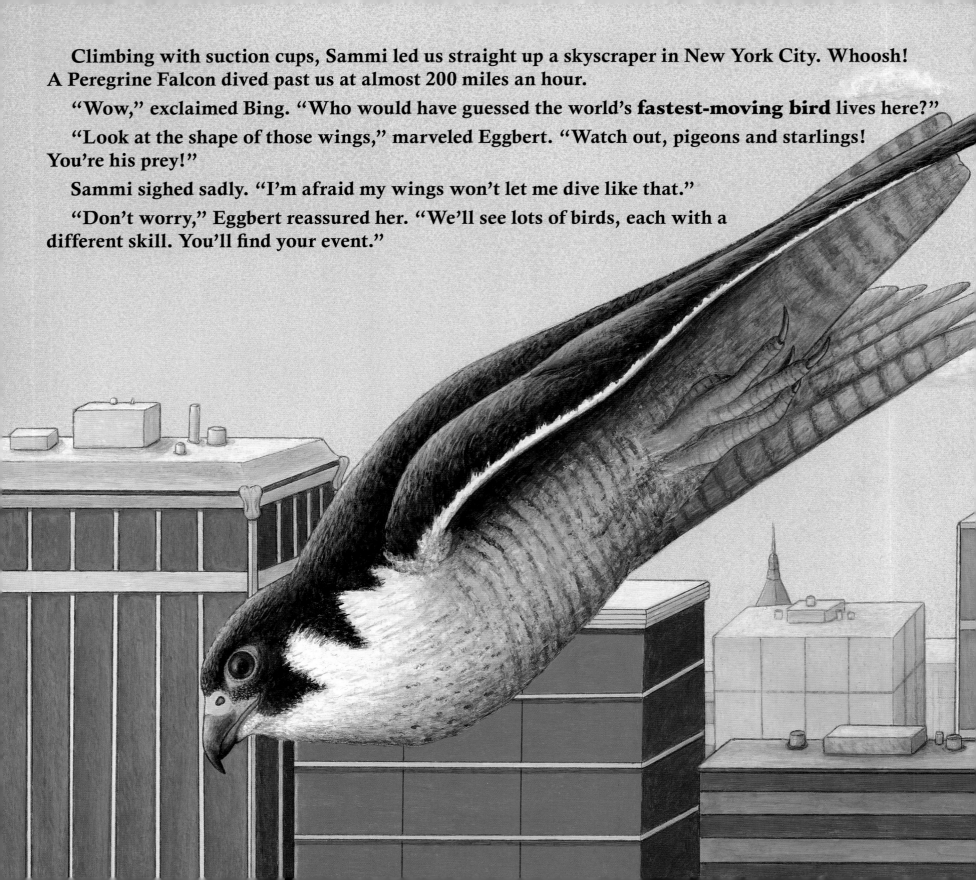

An Extra Extreme! from Eggbert the Expert
Although the falcon is the fastest, a **Red-tailed Hawk** named Pale Male is the **most famous** bird in Ne[w] York City. There are two movies and several books abo[ut] him!

Sammi's Notebook

   The fastest animal on Earth—the Peregrine Falcon! The perfect bird to begin my extreme birding journal.

   Peregrines move the fastest when diving down on prey from high above. Their spectacular dive is called a "stoop." Bing says that's easy to remember because it rhymes with "swoop."

   Falcons that live in the wild build nests on cliffs, but falcons that live in cities build their nests on ledges of tall buildings.

FIELD GUIDE

PEREGRINE FALCON

Body Size: 14-21 in.
Wingspan: 39-43 in.
Habitat: Worldwide where there are cliffs and open areas; also in cities.
Food: Mostly birds; also bats and small mammals.
Sound: Alarm call is a harsh *rehk-rehk-rehk.*

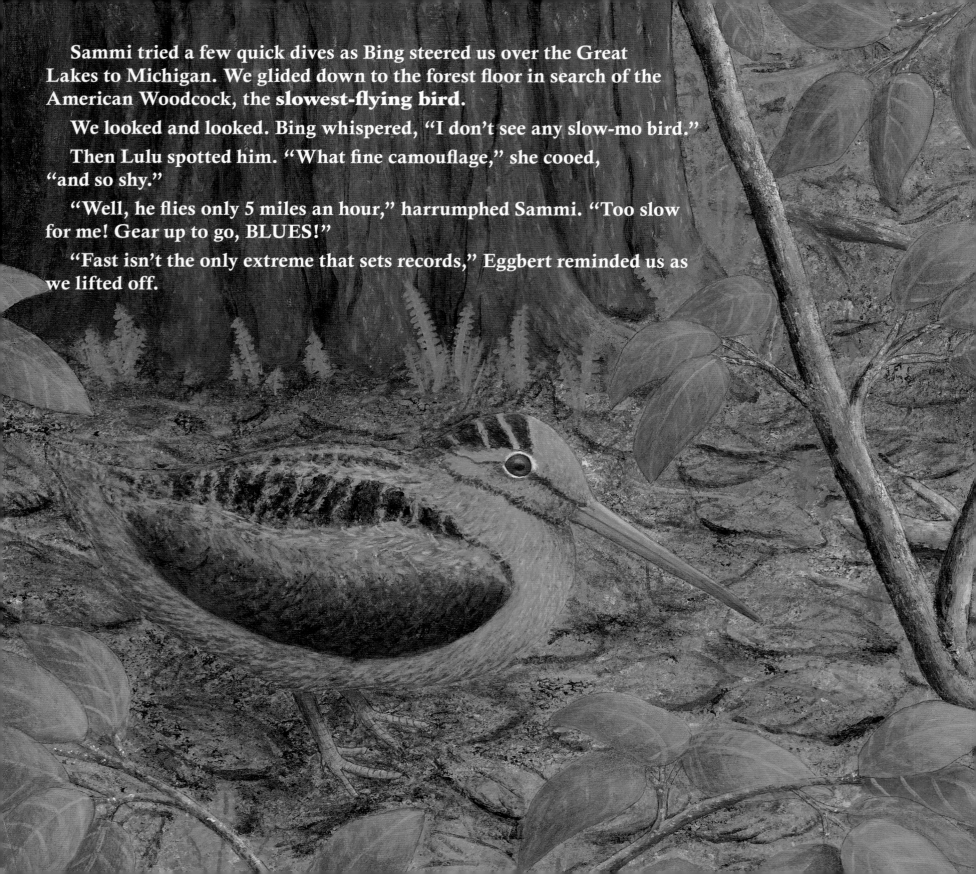

Sammi tried a few quick dives as Bing steered us over the Great Lakes to Michigan. We glided down to the forest floor in search of the American Woodcock, the **slowest-flying bird**.

We looked and looked. Bing whispered, "I don't see any slow-mo bird."

Then Lulu spotted him. "What fine camouflage," she cooed, "and so shy."

"Well, he flies only 5 miles an hour," harrumphed Sammi. "Too slow for me! Gear up to go, BLUES!"

"Fast isn't the only extreme that sets records," Eggbert reminded us as we lifted off.

An Extra Extreme! from Eggbert the Expert
Sammi wasn't impressed with the slowest flier, but I think she would like the **Wandering Albatross**. It has the **largest wingspan**—almost 12 feet! It flies for hours without flapping.

Eggbert's Notebook

We were so lucky to spot the American Woodcock. It was almost invisible as it searched for worms.

But it didn't have any trouble seeing all around—360 degrees. That's the largest field of vision of any bird.

Woodcocks may be the slowest-flying birds, but when frightened they "explode" into the air. And male woodcocks perform a sensational "sky dance" for females.

FIELD GUIDE

AMERICAN WOODCOCK

Body Size: 9-12 in.
Wingspan: 16-20 in.
Habitat: Moist woodlands and meadows.
Food: Earthworms and other invertebrates.
Sound: Mating call is a loud, buzzy *peent*.

An Extra Extreme! from Eggbert the Expert

Although the Arctic tern migrates the longest distance, the **Bar-tailed Godwit** makes the **longest nonstop flight**—a nine-day, 7,000-mile one-way trip from Alaska to New Zealand.

Bing's Notebook

Arctic Terns are mighty marathoners! Their one-way migration almost equals flying once around the Earth. It takes them 90 days—and they don't use a map!

Arctic Terns are the ultimate sun-lovers. They *see* more daylight than any other living creature. How? They alternate between summer in the Arctic and summer in the Antarctic where the sun never sets in the middle of summer.

ARCTIC TERN

Body size: 12-15 in.
Wingspan: 31 in.
Habitat: Arctic tundra, boreal forests, or rocky islands; edge of Antarctic pack ice.
Food: Small fish, shrimp, krill, insects and small invertebrates.
Sound: Short *kip* and a harsh *kee-errr*.

Why me?

Just for fun, we floated in a hot-air balloon over Canada to Alaska, while an Arctic Tern hovered next to us.

"Magnificent!" Eggbert exclaimed. "Look at the grand **champion of long-distance fliers**! He came all the way from Antarctica, and he'll return in the fall—a 22,000 mile trip."

"I'm as determined as a tern," twirped Sammi. "Let's follow his route to Antarctica, even if it takes us days and nights."

Lulu snapped a photo as Bing crooned, "Fly long and strong, hearty BLUES!"

We finally arrived in Antarctica, the coldest place on Earth. "I want to swim with this Emperor Penguin," sang Sammi. "She's the world's **deepest diver**, going down 1800 feet!"

"BRRR," shivered Lulu. "It's cold and dark down there."

"Plah!" Sammi spluttered when she popped up to the surface after only a minute. "Wow! She stayed under for 20 minutes. That's the 'longest time underwater' record too. An extreme athlete for an extreme place."

Looks like a torpedo in a tuxedo.

A-a-a-a-a-air!

I'm turning BLUER! Think pink.

My feet have the blues!

"I-I-I'm an i-i-ice c-c-cube," Uno chattered. "L-L-Let's g-g-go s-s-someplace w-w-warm."

"Right-o, here we go!" agreed Bing, and blew his whistle.

An Extra Extreme! from Eggbert the Expert
The Emperor Penguin dives the deepest, but the **Gentoo Penguin** is the **fastest underwater swimming** bird in the world. It reaches speeds of 22 miles per hour as it hunts for fish and krill.

Lulu's Notebook

The Emperor Penguins didn't seem to mind sub-zero temperatures. A thick layer of body fat was keeping them toasty warm. And their oily, waterproof feathers kept their skin dry. I used a wet suit and pretty pink flippers!

Too bad my camera wasn't waterproof. I would have taken photos of them "flying" through the water. They use their wings like strong paddles to dive down deep for food.

FIELD GUIDE

EMPEROR PENGUIN

Body: 40-48 in.
Wingspan: 30-35 in.
Habitat: Antarctic pack ice.
Food: Fish, squid, and crustaceans.
Sound: Moaning *aaahh, aaahh*.

Uno's Notebook

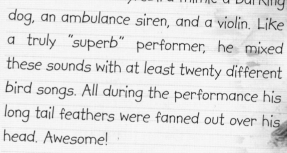

Superb Lyrebirds are super sound experts! They make a steady stream of cool tunes by imitating lots of different sounds.

We heard a lyrebird mimic a barking dog, an ambulance siren, and a violin. Like a truly "superb" performer, he mixed these sounds with at least twenty different bird songs. All during the performance his long tail feathers were fanned out over his head. Awesome!

FIELD GUIDE

SUPERB LYREBIRD

Body Size: 9-10 in.
Tail feathers: 21-24 in.
Habitat: Forests and woods in Australia.
Food: Insects, spiders, beetles, and worms.
Sound: Mimics many sounds; also makes whistles, cackling notes, and a loud alarm call.

We flew north to another record-setting place: Australia, the smallest continent. "The Superb Lyrebird lives here, the **world's best mimic!**" Lulu reminded us. "He's a real beauty too!"

Woof, woof! Whirrrrr! Putt-putt-putt-putt!

"That must be him—the world's greatest copycat!" Bing said. "He copies sounds from all around—other creatures, cars, even chainsaws."

Then the Lyrebird went, *Ah-oooh-oooh!*

"A loony tune," laughed Uno. "He can even imitate an Australian didgeridoo. LET'S JAM!"

We could have played for hours, but Sammi had a schedule to keep.

"G'day mate," we sang out as we departed.

An Extra Extreme! from Eggbert the Expert

Even though the Swift rarely lands, the **Sooty Tern** holds the record as the **most-aerial** bird. It doesn't land for 3 to 4 years! A tropical sea bird, it scoops up fish from the ocean surface when it's hungry.

Sammi's Notebook

The White-throated Needletail Swift is a "winged wonder." With wings swept back in a curve, it looks like a boomerang whizzing across the sky. It even sleeps in the air!

I love it because it's extremely f-a-s-t — the fastest bird in **flapping flight**! It's sort of like one of my other favorites, the Peregrine Falcon, the **fastest bird when it dives**.

FIELD GUIDE

WHITE-THROATED NEEDLETAIL SWIFT

Body Size: 7.5-9 in.

Habitat: Dense old-growth forests; rocky hills.

Food: Flying insects, such as termites, beetles, and flies.

Sound: *Chitter-chitter-chitter.*

Flies on the fly-by!

Umm ... What about potty breaks?

Ugh, a bug!

"Fly in formation, BLUES!" urged Sammi, as she pointed us toward Siberia. We were getting in shape, but it was an extreme challenge.

SWOOOOSH. Something whizzed past.

"Was that a boomerang?" shouted Bing. "Or an incredibly swift bird?"

"Bingo, Bing!" congratulated Eggbert. "That's the White-throated Needletail Swift, the **fastest-level-flying** champion. He sets the record at 105 mph! He hardly ever lands—he eats and drinks in flight."

"Swift for sure," grumbled Uno, "but I can't lift another feather."

We headed for the Himalaya Mountains at dawn.
We struggled against fierce winds on Mount Everest,
the highest mountain on Earth.

A Bar-headed Goose flew overhead. "Amazing!
How can it breathe up there?" gasped Lulu into thin air.
"We're at 29,000 feet—over five miles above sea level!"

Eggbert proclaimed, "There's the **highest-flying bird** in the
world! When it migrates between India and Tibet, it flies
50 miles per hour and covers 1,000 miles in a day."

"Go, goose, go!" Sammi chanted.

"Go, BLUES, go!" signaled Bing, and we took off.

Bing's Notebook

Flyin' high in the sky, Bar-headed Geese go high as they please.

They're such powerful flappers they can stay on course even when battered by gusty mountain crosswinds.

Their constant flapping creates lots of body heat, which is held in by their down feathers. This helps prevent ice from forming on their wings as they migrate over frozen mountaintops.

FIELD GUIDE

BAR-HEADED GOOSE

Body Size: 30 in.
Wingspan: 55-66 in.
Habitat: High mountain lakes and areas with short grass.
Food: Grass, wheat, barley, and rice.
Sound: Low honking.

Our wings de-iced as we flew to England, arriving at night. But no sleep for us—just another workout! "Headlamps on!" Sammi coached. "Climbing ropes ready! Up we go!"

Suddenly a Barn Owl swooped over the field below, swiftly grabbed a mouse, and silently flew off.

"Eeeew," whined Lulu. "How could the owl see him? It's pitch black out here."

"He heard it," Eggbert replied. "The Barn Owl has the **keenest hearing** of any bird."

Sammi listened really hard but heard only snoring. Uno was fast asleep.

An Extra Extreme! from Eggbert the Expert
The Barn Owl has keen hearing, and like all raptors it also has excellent vision. Another raptor, the **Bald Eagle**, has such **sharp eyesight** it can see a mouse from over a mile away.

Eggbert's Notebook

The "heart" around a Barn Owl's face is formed by stiff feathers. These feathers focus sounds toward the owl's ears. One ear is higher than the other, which helps the owl pinpoint exactly where sounds are coming from.

Barn Owls can capture a mouse in total darkness, just using sound to precisely locate their prey.

When I get home, I'll go online to watch barn owl eggs hatch at Cornell Lab's NestWatch.

FIELD GUIDE

BARN OWL

Body Size: 12.5-15.5 in.

Wing Span: 39.5-42 in.

Habitat: Open areas, such as grasslands, deserts, marshes, and fields.

Food: Small mammals, such as voles, shrews, and mice.

Sound: Drawn out hissing scream.

"Another day, another continent," Bing crooned as we started our African safari and met several ostriches.

"The Ostrich is the **fastest-running bird** in the world!" reported Eggbert. "He's also the tallest and heaviest bird with the biggest eyes."

"Listen to him boom and snort. Quite a guy, but he can't fly," Bing rhymed.

"Check out those big, strong legs," sang Sammi. "He can cover 16 feet with each stride and can kill a lion with a single kick. He's a whiz on the track, but not in the air."

Twweeeeeeet! Bing's whistle again. "Time to cruise, BLUES."

An Extra Extreme! from Eggbert the Expert
Like the ostrich, the **Emu** of Australia is big and unable to fly. It holds the record for the **longest distance walked** by a migrating bird—320 miles.

Sammi's Notebook

Gotta love a bird that sets so many records! Ostriches are nine feet tall, can weigh over 250 pounds, and lay the largest eggs of any bird. It takes about 24 chicken eggs to weigh as much as just one ostrich egg—over 3 pounds. And guess what? Several ostrich mothers share one nest. We saw a "big mama" protecting a nest with over 40 eggs.

FIELD GUIDE

OSTRICH

Body Size: 7–9.25 ft.

Wing Span: 6.6 ft.

Habitat: African savannas and deserts.

Food: Mostly plant roots, leaves, and seeds; also eat insects and small animals, such as lizards.

Sound: A booming call; also whistles and snorts.

Lulu's Notebook

As we flew to Tanzania I was delighted to see a pink sea. Then I realized I wasn't looking at water, but thousands of Greater Flamingos!

Eggbert told me flamingos are pink because of the food they eat. They lower their bills upside-down into the shallow lake and move them back and forth to filter out shrimp and algae.

Yuck! Even for pink feathers I wouldn't dip my beak into that muddy water.

FIELD GUIDE

GREATER FLAMINGO

Body Size: 36-50 in.

Wing Span: 55-65 in.

Habitat: Warm, shallow, salty lakes and lagoons.

Food: Protozoa, algae, brine-shrimp, and insects.

Sound: Gooselike calls, gabbling, honking, grunting and growling.

Uno, *you're* backwards.

Our next African stop was Lake Manyara, a salty lake in Tanzania and a favorite place for animals.

"I'm tickled pink," giggled Lulu as we windsurfed among thousands of Greater Flamingos—the **world's pinkest** birds. "My idols! How do they stay so perfectly pink?"

Sammi sang, "This is fun!" as she skimmed back and forth with perfect balance. "See, one leg, just like them!"

"It's Sammi the Super Surfer!" Bing teased. "There's lots more water ahead. Over the ocean we go!"

What a daredevil duo!

Bing

Eggbert

Sammi was eager to try whitewater sports, but Uno was homesick. Bing coaxed him all the way to a rushing mountain stream in South America.

"UH-OH!" Uno cried above the roar of the rapids. "A baby ducky just fell into the torrent! There goes another one!"

Eggbert smiled. "They didn't fall, Uno. They jumped! Those baby Torrent Ducks are among the **boldest chicks** in the world! But their downy feathers keep them afloat."

"What a courageous team!" exclaimed Sammi. "Hmmm . . . you know what? So are we, BLUES!"

An Extra Extreme! from Eggbert the Expert
Torrent Duck chicks are incredibly courageous and so are **Common Murre chicks**. When only a month old, they **bravely leap** from cliffs to the ocean below.

Uno's Notebook

Rubber Ducky will never believe this. I saw two brave little Torrent Duck chicks leap right into the raging whitewater.

Phew! I was so relieved when the ducklings popped up out of the foam. They acted like it was "no big deal" and happily paddled to a still spot near shore. That's where I wanted to be too!

They're downy, I'm drowny!

I want them on my team.

oun

Sammi

Lulu

FIELD GUIDE

TORRENT DUCK

Body Size: 16–18 in
Habitat: Streams and rivers of the Andes mountains.
Food: Mostly stonefly larvae.
Sound: A shrill *weet*; male makes a sharp whistle and female makes raspy *quack*.

An Extra Extreme! from Eggbert the Expert
While the Sungem Hummingbird has the fastest wingbeat, another hummingbird— the **Bee Hummingbird** of Cuba—is the **smallest** bird. It's only 2 1/4 inches long and weighs less than a penny.

Sammi's Notebook

Hummingbirds don't "hum," but their wings move so fast that it sounds like it. The Horned Sungem has the fastest wings of all.

What acrobatic aviators! Hummers can fly in any direction—right, left, up, down, backwards, even upside down—and hover in mid-air.

They may be tiny, but they're mighty record-setters, with the smallest eggs, smallest nests, and the fewest feathers of any bird. Plus they're the smallest warm-blooded animals on Earth.

FIELD GUIDE

HORNED SUNGEM HUMMINGBIRD

Body Size: 3.5-4.3 in.
Habitat: Grasslands and forests along rivers in Brazil.
Food: Nectar of flowering bushes and trees; also insects.
Sound: High-pitched *chip chip*.

We found our final record-setting bird while still in South America—the tiny Horned Sungem Hummingbird.

"Look at those magnificent feathers," Lulu whispered. "They sparkle in the sun like gems!"

"This hummingbird **beats its wings faster** than any other bird," said Eggbert. "Ninety times every second! That's over 5,000 beats a minute."

Sammi was thoughtful as she watched the hummer zip around. "Maybe my event should be the zipline," she mused.

"Well, BLUES, we've finished our list!" declared Bing. "Ready, set, HOME."

Our return trip took us over Brazil. "This famous rainforest holds the world record for **greatest variety of birds**," Eggbert observed. "Let's stop, look, and listen!"

Colorful birds surrounded us—everywhere! Bing just had to sing.

High and low. Fast and slow. What a show!

Black and white, rainbow bright. Such delight!

Lulu's beak fell open with wonder. "What a magical place," she chirped. "A photo op paradise! Can we come back soon? Every bird is different. And each one is so special."

"That's it!" Sammi shouted. "I've got it! My extreme sport! I should have known it all along. Flap up to the airstream, Dream Team! *Now* we're ready to fly home."

We returned home in top shape from our world tour. Uno played with Rubber Ducky in the sand box.

Bing asked Sammi, "So what is your sport? Sammi the Super Surfer?"

"Yeah," Eggbert chimed in. "You've seen extreme bird champions do their thing. What will *you* do?"

"I've decided . . ." Sammi said as she took a deep breath, "that Extreme Birding is my event—OUR event, BLUES! Each bird we saw was a different kind of champion. We're champions, too, because we're awesome birders! Let's ALL enter as *TEAM BLUES BIRD WATCHERS*!"

"Hurray!" cheered Lulu. "An extreme sport with my best friends."

"We're on!" whooped Sammi. "High five, TEAM BLUES. We ARE the best!"

Asia

Australia

Remind me to bring my umbrella.

Bing's Notebook

We traveled all around the world to find record-setting birds. What a long trip! We visited every continent and marked the places where we stopped on our map. Some of the birds we saw can be seen on other continents too, especially those that migrate long distances.

Where We Saw the Champions
- Peregrine Falcon—**New York City**
- American Woodcock—**Michigan**
- Arctic Tern—**Alaska**
- Emperor Penguin—**Antarctica**
- Superb Lyrebird—**Australia**
- White-throated Needletail Swift—**Siberia**
- Bar-headed Goose—**Himalaya Mountains**
- Barn Owl—**England**
- Ostrich—**Central Africa**
- Greater Flamingo—**Tanzania**
- Torrent Duck—**Andes Mountains**
- Horned Sungem Hummingbird—**Brazil**

Just Look Up

Open the door, go outside. You'll see birds everywhere!

- **Children and Nature Network**— Provides news, inspiration, and practical suggestions for parents, educators, and organizations. www.childrenandnature.org
- **Green Hour**—The National Wildlife Federation recommends that parents give their kids a "Green Hour" every day. Discover the inspiration and tools to make the outdoors a part of daily life. www.greenhour.org

Have More Fun with Birds

Find interesting and fun information, projects, birding tips, resources, and curriculum for kids, teachers, and parents:

- Audubon Society www.audubon.org
- Cornell Lab of Ornithology www.birds.cornell.edu
- Bird Watcher's Digest www.birdwatchersdigest.com
- American Birding Assn. www.aba.org
- Birders World www.birdersworld.com

Get a Closer Look

Over 100 species of birds in North America get some of their food from bird feeders. Experience the thrill of watching birds up close when they visit a feeder in your backyard. Birds also need sources of clean water and nesting sites, including nest boxes. Get all the information and products you need to attract birds at bird stores like Wild Birds Unlimited, www.wbu.com, or Wild Bird Center, www.wildbirds.com. Then join Cornell Lab's Project FeederWatch or NestWatch and share your observations with scientists. www.birds.cornell.edu/pfw/

About the Bird-Lovers Who Wrote and Illustrated This Book

CAROL L. MALNOR
Nature Book Lady

Favorite color: All shades of blue

Carol loves
- going birding
- writing books
- doing Tai Chi

Favorite expression:
"Mistakes are wonderful opportunities to learn."

Carol lives with her husband in the foothills of the Sierra Nevada, where she has breakfast with her backyard birds each morning.

SANDY F. FULLER
Kid-at-Heart

Favorite color: Blue (It's true!)

Sandy loves
- family and friends
- mountains and Maine
- guitars and gourmet

Favorite expression:
"FAR OUT!"

Sandy lives in Colorado, sharing mountain life with Riva (golden retriever), Ellsworth (aka Bill) and Scott and Kimberly (when they visit Mom!).

LOUISE SCHROEDER
World Traveler

Favorite color: Aquamarine

Louise loves
- being with family
- enjoying nature
- painting

Favorite expression:
"Let's go somewhere."

A native of rural Canada and visual creator of the Blues, Louise lives with her husband and three daughters in Austin, Texas.

The BLUES invite parents, teachers, and kids to visit them at www.thebluesgobirding.com. You'll discover great birding resources, lesson plans, backyard bird watching tips, citizen science projects, coloring pages, and more.

Dawn Publications is dedicated to inspiring in children a deeper understanding and appreciation for all life on Earth. You can browse through our titles, download resources for teachers, and order at www.dawnpub.com, or call 800-545-7475.